TEMPLE RUN
RUN FOR YOUR LIFE! ™

PYRAMID PERIL

EGMONT
Publishing
NEW YORK

With special thanks to Adrian Bott.

EGMONT
We bring stories to life

First published in the United Kingdom by Egmont UK Limited, 2015
First published in the United States of America by Egmont Publishing, 2015
443 Park Avenue South, Suite 806
New York, NY 10016
Cover illustration by Jacopo Camagni
Interior illustrations by Artful Doodlers
Text & illustrations copyright © 2015 Imangi Studios, LLC
All Rights Reserved
1 3 5 7 9 8 6 4 2
www.ImangiStudios.com
www.egmontusa.com
ISBN 978-1-60684-594-3
eBook ISBN 978-1-60684-595-0

Printed in the United States of America

Everyone's heard of Zack Wonder, the football star. He's one of the richest athletes around, and one of the most generous, too.

Nobody knows how many good causes he donates to, but there are rumors he's given away millions. Other players like to dine at fancy restaurants, but Zack would just as soon make a peanut butter sandwich and send the check to a charity instead.

Now everyone's crazy about his new project, a kids' TV show that looks into cool, strange, historical facts and locations. He's calling it *Wonders of the Universe*. Two weeks ago, he announced he was looking for a host for a special episode in Egypt.

When the contest was announced, you sent your name in. What did you have to lose? But then the email from Zack Wonder came, and you nearly had a heart attack!

You yelled for your parents to come in and read it, but it wasn't a hoax. It really was from Zack Wonder himself. Here's what it said:

WONDERS OF THE UNIVERSE

CONGRATULATIONS! You're the winner of my **Search for a Star** contest. Out of thousands of competition entries, I've picked YOURS. We're going to Egypt, Land of the Pharaohs, together!

There's a new tomb that's just been discovered. No one has set foot in there ever since it was built. We'll be the first people inside. Hope you're not scared of small, cramped spaces!

I've picked you because I think I can rely on you. I need someone who's cool under pressure, who loves history, and who has that special magic spark on camera. If you impress me enough, maybe we can work together again. No promises.

You won't be going alone. I'm bringing some experts. There'll be explorer Guy Dangerous—you probably know his show, *Whatever It Takes*—and our cultural guide, Karma Lee, who speaks a dozen different languages.

Your friend,

Zack Wonder

Zack has sent some files for you to look through. They tell you all about the tomb. According to reports, the outside of the tomb has features no archaeologist has ever seen before, including carvings of a weird, monkey-like demon.

What could this mean, you wonder?

You're about to find out . . .

★

The tomb you're going to explore is in the middle of the desert. Luckily, Zack's booked you into a fancy new hotel in a nearby town.

Zack meets you on the hotel steps, grins, and shakes your hand. Cameras flash all around you.

"Hey, Zack!" yells a reporter. "Who's the kid?"

"My host," Zack tells him. Suddenly, everyone wants a picture of you. Zack quickly leads you into the hotel. "Come on in. You must be tired."

"I'm not tired," you explain, waving at the cameras as you head inside. You've never been on TV before. "I'm excited!"

Zack looks happy. "That's the spirit!"

4

It turns out Zack's rented the entire dining room of the hotel for the pre-shoot party. A crowd has already gathered. Important-looking people are peering at screens flashing information about the tomb, the show, and Zack's plans for the future. Everywhere you look, you see men in expensive suits and women in evening gowns and jewelry. You must be the youngest person here.

You notice two people giving an interview for the news cameras. One is also American, a guy with thick red hair, and the other is a Chinese woman with her hair up. She notices you and calls you over. "Guy! Look who made it!"

The man pats you on the shoulder. "Good to meet you. I'm Guy Dangerous. This is Karma Lee, my glamorous assistant."

Karma smiles sweetly. "Assistant, indeed! Guy loves his little jokes."

"Behave yourself around Karma," Guy warns you. "She's got a kick like an Alabama mule."

"Don't mind Guy," Karma says, squeezing

your hand. "He's all right really."

Zack comes over, looking pleased. "So my team's all here. Cool. I want you folks to have a good time tonight. Kick back, eat, mingle. Tomorrow, it's the grand tomb opening. Make sure you're all there."

"Tomorrow?" Guy protests. "We should head down there right now! Why wait?"

"The tomb's been there for thousands of years, Guy," says Karma. "It can wait a few more hours. I say we head down to the market."

"You just want to go shopping."

"Yeah, for antique swords!" Karma says, rolling her eyes. "And statues, and relics . . ."

As you enjoy the food and talk to the celebrity guests, you notice a slender red-haired woman in sunglasses watching you from the shadows. She has an electronic device in her hand. As you watch, she scans the room with it, then quickly tucks it away.

Who is she? you wonder. *Some kind of spy, maybe?* The next moment, she's disappeared.

After a brief press conference, Zack calls you over

again. "It's decision time," he says. "I've spoken to Guy and Karma, and they both want to do different things, so I'm leaving the choice in your hands."

Zack explains: Do you want to go and explore the tomb right away with Guy? Or would you rather wait and go explore the local market with Karma, and get some footage of the town?

Guy Dangerous is excited to go and explore the tomb now, now, *now.* "Who cares if it's late?" he says. "The security guards at the tomb have seen interlopers lurking around—they could be tomb robbers! It's important to get in there before someone else sneaks in and ransacks the place!"

Karma Lee is much more interested in exploring the markets, to see the cool artifacts and exotic weapons on offer. She laughs off Guy's suggestion that the tomb is at risk of thieves.

Just then, the mysterious red-haired woman appears again, watching you from a balcony. You realize you have a third choice. You could pull Zack off to one side and tell him about her. Whoever this

person is, she's not Egyptian, she's got some weird electronic thingamajig, and she's acting like she's got something to hide.

What are you going to do?

The tomb could be exciting, and it *is* why you came here. To go with Guy, head to page 52.

But you can always go to the tomb tomorrow, right? The markets sound amazing. To go with Karma Lee, head to page 8.

To go tell Zack Wonder about the mystery woman, head to page 106.

"You're sure about this?" asks Guy, looking sad. "We could be exploring a tomb, and you want to go to a market instead?"

"Zip it," Karma laughs. "You'll get your tomb adventure soon enough. We've got sights to see. Come on!"

She tucks her hair under a headscarf—"You don't have to wear one, but it's polite!"—and leads you down into the crowded streets of the town. Two members of the film crew follow you: Steve, the cameraman, and Duke, the sound guy. Guy waves to you from the hotel steps. "See you at the dig!"

Steve tracks you with his camera as you weave in and out of the crowds. "Just forget we're here, OK?" he says. "You don't have to perform or anything. Act natural." Duke hurries along behind him, holding a boom mike and grumbling.

There's so much going on here! Car horns blare and people shout for your attention. You pass fabric-sellers, boys shining shoes, and coffee shops where old men are playing backgammon. The smell of fragrant smoke is head-spinning.

Karma asks a smiling man for directions to the *souk*, or bazaar. He's happy to help. He seems to be happy about everything. Steve and Duke get plenty of footage. Karma pays him and excitedly pulls you onward through the street. "We're almost there!"

"Why'd you give that guy money for directions?" you ask her.

"*Baksheesh*," Karma says.

"Bless you?" you reply.

She laughs. "No, *baksheesh* helps things work for you. It's kind of a tip, but not really. It's more 'share and share alike.' Better get used to it."

When you arrive at the *souk*, the sights and sounds take your breath away. There are carpets for sale, books, statuettes, jewelry, food that smells amazing— even tourist stuff like gold plastic Tutankhamen heads and a snow globe of the Pyramids.

Karma grins at that. "They must have made the globe because it actually snowed on the Pyramids a few years ago," she says.

Farther along, you see a stall with figurines of Egyptian gods. There's Isis, the mother goddess, and dog-headed Anubis, guardian of tombs. It's funny to think people believed in these guys for thousands of years. Anubis looks fierce. You hope he's not waiting for you in that tomb tomorrow.

Karma buys a little statue of Bes, the god of luck. He's short, fat, and is sticking out his tongue. "Present for you," she says, passing Bes over. "For good luck."

"Thanks!"

You spend some time checking out an amazing selection of colorful, fascinating goods. Karma goes all starry-eyed over a replica of an ancient ceremonial battle ax. Steve gets some excellent footage and even Duke seems happy at last.

Just as you're thinking how cool this all is, you notice a stubbly-faced guy standing at an antiquities stall. His eyes are narrow and mean-looking. You're sure he's up to something.

"Karma, check him out," you say in a low voice.

Karma glances at him and gasps. "It can't be. What's he doing here?"

"You know him?"

"I know *of* him. That's Montana Smith, the world's second most famous explorer!"

Montana Smith is looking very closely at a strange golden mask. The mask looks out of place here, like it's not Egyptian at all. Meanwhile, the trader frowns at him and says something angry in Egyptian Arabic.

12

The next second, Montana grabs the mask! He runs off through the crowd.

The trader lunges for him and misses. He falls sprawling across his stall.

You have to stop Montana! Without thinking, you start running after him. "Hey! Stop!"

Karma sees what's happening and dashes after you. The chase is on! Poor Steve and Duke are left in the dust as you race off in pursuit.

Montana looks over his shoulder, sees you chasing him, and ducks down an alley.

You need to make a quick decision. Is it better for Karma to come down the alley with you for safety in numbers? Or should she run around to the other end of the alley and block it off so Montana will be trapped?

To run down the alley with Karma, dash to page 87.

To send Karma around to the other end of the alley and cut Montana off, head to page 24.

You take a running leap and land with a THUMP! on the back of the cab. Montana wasn't expecting *that*. His eyes widen as you bash on the rear window, trying to hammer your way in.

The cab driver realizes what you're up to and swerves the car, trying to throw you off. White cracks start to show in the window glass. One good hard whack and you'll be through!

Then the cab driver slams on the brakes. You go flying over the car and land heavily in the dust. *Oof!*

The bad news is that Montana gets away. The *really* bad news is that you twist your ankle. You get to spend the rest of your time in Egypt in a nice clean hospital bed. Oh well, at least the view is cool . . .

The next morning, Zack comes to see you. It turns out your little adventure was caught on camera! Zack's so impressed that he makes you his full-time cohost. Who says there are no happy endings anymore?

RUN AGAIN? TURN TO PAGE **4**

14

You and Karma dive into a second cab and chase Montana through the hot Egyptian night. You're gaining on him!

Then, to your dismay, you reach an intersection. Montana's cab shoots across, leaving you on the other side just as the lights change.

"Get after him!" you yell.

The driver shakes his head. He's not going to run a red light.

Moments later, there's total gridlock as the oncoming traffic fills up the available space. You grind your teeth—this is frustrating! Do you get out and sprint over to Montana, or stay in the cab and hope your driver can catch up?

To sprint through the stopped traffic to Montana, run to page 22.

To sit tight and wait, go to page 23.

This is crazy, you think as you leap on to the bike—but it just might work.

The bike's owner comes out of the shop and yells at you. You holler that you'll give it back afterward, promise! Karma gives him a fistful of money. Shouts go up all around you. Suddenly, everyone in the street has a bike to sell.

Karma kicks off and starts pedaling like mad, while you hang on tightly to the back of the bike.

You chase Montana's cab through the traffic, weaving in and out of oncoming cars. The driver tries to pull away from you, but the strength in Karma Lee's legs is amazing and she just keeps pedaling. She won't give up without a fight. You hang on for dear life. If you fell off the bike at this speed, you'd make a nasty mess on the road!

The cab drives out of town down a big main road and picks up the pace. Your heart sinks—surely there's no way to catch Montana now. Even Karma Lee can't pedal a bike at eighty miles an hour.

But just as you think he's going to escape, the cab

pulls over with a screech of brakes and stops outside a huge walled estate. Montana climbs out, still clutching the mask, and staggers toward the gates.

Karma brings the bicycle to a skidding halt and sags across the handlebars, gasping. But she's not ready to give up. "Come on, let's get him!"

Montana pushes through the open gates and runs inside. You follow him, only moments behind. The mansion is set in a garden the size of a park. Montana runs around the side, heading for the back.

You can't imagine why Montana would run for shelter in a place like this, but you don't think the owner would approve. Which way now? Do you bang on the front door and ask for help, or follow Montana around the back?

To run around to the back after Montana, head to page 29.

To knock on the front door, head to page 26.

Y ou look up and down the street, but there's no sign of Montana. Karma sighs. "He got away."

"What a jerk!" you mutter. "Let's head back and talk to the stall guy. We might need to go to the police."

You make your way back through the market to the stall where Montana grabbed the mask. The Egyptian police are there already. To your surprise, they're leading the market trader away in handcuffs!

You run up to them. "Wait! This guy isn't a thief! A guy stole a mask from *him* and ran away."

Karma Lee doesn't need to translate, because the policeman speaks excellent English. "You are mistaken, my young friend," he says sadly. "This man is a thief. Worse, he is a tomb robber. The mask you saw was stolen from a dig near here."

Karma gasps. "Not the new tomb?"

He nods, and she turns to you. "That's the tomb you're supposed to be exploring with Guy tomorrow! Montana Smith must have realized the mask was something special. He's always been good at spotting artifacts."

The pair of you go to the police station to give your statement. It's a long, uncomfortable wait in a hot room. When you're finally done, you head back to the hotel, only to see a sad-faced Zack Wonder waiting for you on the hotel steps.

"We're going to have to call off the show," he says. "Someone beat us into the tomb. Slipped past security and headed straight for a secret room deep inside. It's like he knew exactly where to go."

"Let me guess," Karma says. "Montana Smith."

"That's his name all right. Eyewitnesses say he came running out of the tomb like the devil was after him!"

You're pretty disappointed to have missed such an amazing opportunity, but Zack tells you not to worry. You'll just have to go and shoot your show somewhere else. Did you know they've just found a hidden chamber under Stonehenge? Better get your bags packed!

RUN AGAIN? TURN TO PAGE **4**

You hurry down the alleyway and take a better look at the drainpipe. It's hanging half off the wall. The fastenings have been pulled out.

Hold on—the patches of damage to the wall are still crumbly! This must have happened recently. Maybe someone climbed up the pipe and their weight pulled it away from the brickwork?

Encouraged, and feeling a little like Sherlock Holmes, you look for more clues. You notice a bootprint on the wall above your head. That proves it. Montana Smith scrambled up this drainpipe only moments ago. He must be running over the rooftops!

"He's up on the roof!" you shout to Karma.

Karma Lee laces her fingers together to make a step for you. "I'll give you a boost."

You step up and grab the pipe. Karma hoists you up so hard that you almost shoot through the air. It's easy for you to scramble up the last few feet like a monkey and pull yourself up on to the flat roof. There's Montana, sprinting away. You were right!

"I see him!" you yell triumphantly. "Get up here."

Karma tries to follow you up, but she's too heavy. The moment she puts her weight on the drainpipe, the whole thing cracks off the wall and falls into the alley with a crash. You wince.

"I'll follow from the ground!" Karma hollers. As you turn to chase Montana, she adds, "Don't let him out of your sight."

You start running across the wide, flat rooftop. Montana has already reached the far edge, and now he's leaping from one roof to the next! It's a long way to jump. He lands hard and almost drops the mask, but he makes it. You have to get him, but how? That jump looks scary.

You glance around and see an old plank lying among some decayed rope and cans of paint. You could try laying the plank across the gap and carefully walking across it. Or you could just try the jump and give it all you've got.

To walk across the plank, step on to page 36.

To try jumping the gap, leap to page 28.

Y ou try the door, but it's locked. The sounds of shouting from behind it are getting louder.

The door doesn't look too sturdy. Maybe you should play the action movie hero and try to kick it open?

Or, if you don't want to be quite so violent, you could always investigate the drainpipe near the end of the alley, or run back into the street and see if Montana's there.

To kick the door open as hard as you can, go to page 41.

To check out the drainpipe, run to page 19.

To run back into the street, zoom to page 17.

Y ou run out of the cab. You jump across the cars. Drivers yell and shake their fists.

Montana sees you coming with Karma Lee close behind, and has no choice but to dive out of the cab and start running again.

You chase him on foot, getting closer and closer, until you reach a huge building out of town. It's some sort of mansion—someone wealthy must live here. Maybe an athlete or a movie star, you guess.

Montana runs up to an open front window, jumps in, and slams the window down.

You've got two choices. You could bang on the front door and let the people in the house know there's an intruder inside. Or you could run around to the back of the house and look for a way in, so you can catch him yourself.

Do you bang on the door? Turn to page 26.

Or run around to the back of the house?
Turn to page 29.

Y ou wait, and wait, and wait. Eventually, the traffic clears and your driver is able to start chasing Montana again.

To your delight, you catch sight of him. "There he is!" you yell. You zoom down the dusty roads, heading out of town. Your cab screeches around corners and swerves to avoid pedestrians. It looks like the cab driver is getting into the spirit of the chase. It's like being in an action movie!

Unfortunately, this *isn't* an action movie. Just as you're about to pull up alongside Montana, your driver takes a corner too fast and you slam into a pile of chicken crates.

Squawk! You spend the rest of your trip in the hospital, being thoroughly checked over.

RUN AGAIN? TURN TO PAGE **4**

"Karma, go that way!" you yell.

She nods. "Got it." With her fast legs, she should make it there before Montana does.

You run into the alley, certain that the two of you will trap Montana between you.

However, you can't see him anywhere. The only person you see is Karma, who's run all the way around and comes up to meet you in the middle of the alley.

"Where'd he go?" Karma asks, confused.

"I don't know," you admit. You look up, down, and around, but Montana has disappeared into thin air!

"Well, he couldn't have teleported away, could he?" Karma says. "Not unless that mask was magic . . ."

You don't bother wasting any time on that suggestion. Montana must be here somewhere.

You spin around, thinking quickly. Montana might have made it back to the main street somehow, and tried to lose himself among the crowds. You could run back and see if you can spot him there. Or he might have opened one of the doors along

the length of the alley and dived
through it.

You can hear what
sounds like shouting
coming from behind the
nearest door. Maybe he's
inside?

A little farther down,
there's a drainpipe hanging
off the wall. It looks pretty
loose and difficult to climb,
but maybe you should check
it out anyway?

You've only got time
to do one of these things. Think fast!

If you run back into the street,
sprint to page 17.

To try the wooden door, dash to page 21.

To investigate the loose drainpipe,
rush to page 19.

A hollow-cheeked butler in a spotless black uniform answers the door. He looks you up and down. "Can I help you?"

"There's a man," you gasp, fighting for breath. "He stole a mask back at the market, and he ran off, and we've been chasing him, and now he's here . . ."

The butler looks at you as if you'd just said you had crashed your spaceship and needed some power crystals to get it going again. "I beg your pardon?"

Karma takes over the story. "We've been chasing a man named Montana Smith . . ."

As Karma explains, you look past the butler into the house. It's an amazing place. Green ferns sit in huge pots, and enormous portraits hang on the walls. Glass cases in the entrance hall display Egyptian relics, as if this was a mini museum. You can see all the way through to the French windows at the back, which are opened to the gardens.

The butler doesn't look very impressed with Karma's story. "Perhaps I should search the house?"

he says, sounding sarcastic. "We might have pirates in the cellar."

You don't have time for this. Montana Smith can't get away with his theft because of a snooty butler! It would be pretty easy to just shove past him and into the house. Then you could catch Montana and prove you were telling the truth. Or you could give up on the butler entirely, and run around the back.

To push your way in, head to page 34.

To run around the back, sprint to page 29.

You time the jump perfectly. Montana glances back at you and mutters a curse. You leap over another gap between houses, hot on his heels. This is fun!

You end up on the roof of a large building. Montana crashes through a skylight and drops down into the room below.

Follow him to page 33.

You scramble over a wooden fence, sprint across the lawn, and see Montana Smith dashing ahead in front of you.

He's running toward a swimming pool. Wow, that water looks good right now—you're all hot and sweaty from your run. You wonder if Montana's planning to dive-bomb into it, and decide to do the same if he does.

Beside the pool, an Egyptian woman in sunglasses is sitting reading a magazine. She leaps to her feet and shouts, "All of you, stop! What is the meaning of this?"

You, Karma, and—to your surprise—Montana all stop running. Montana looks like a kid who's been shouted at by a teacher.

Karma Lee nudges you. "I know who that lady is! She's Safia Shaarawi."

You remember that name. Zack Wonder mentioned her. She's a famous archeologist and supporter of museums.

"Ma'am, that man is a thief!" you tell her, pointing

to Montana. "That mask he's carrying? He stole it from the market!"

"I hope that's not true," Safia says coldly, "or he'll be spending a long time in jail. Well? What have you got to say for yourself, Mr. . . . ?"

"The name's Smith!" Montana drawls. "And I ain't no thief. The guy running the market stall, he was the thief. I was stealing this mask back!"

Everyone stares. "What?" says Karma.

Safia claps her hands and a butler comes running. "I think we'd better have some tea," she says. "It seems we have a lot to talk about."

Everyone calms down a bit. You talk things through. Montana explains that the mask is a precious relic called the Face of the Idol. The moment he saw it, he realized no regular trader could have something so rare for sale.

"It must have been stolen," he explains. "Stolen from the same dig that uncovered that new tomb."

"The tomb I'm supposed to be exploring tomorrow!" you say.

"So the market traders you snatched it from were relic robbers?" gasps Karma.

Montana nods. "Trying to sell the mask for a quick profit. I told you I wasn't no thief. This mask belongs in a museum!"

"So why come to my house?" Safia asks.

"I was bringing the mask to you for safekeeping, ma'am. I figured you'd know what to do with it."

Safia laughs. "It seems this has all been one big misunderstanding. Thank you, Mr. Smith. Thank you very much. Perhaps you'd like to go indoors and freshen up?"

Once Montana's out of the way, Safia takes you to one side and explains that the new tomb is rumored to have a priceless golden idol in it. "If you happen to find it," she says, "please ensure it ends up on display in a museum—not in some corporation's safe. There are thieves everywhere," she warns. "Be careful."

You feel even more excited about exploring the tomb with Guy tomorrow.

To Karma's delight, Safia even agrees to take part in the TV show you're making. Soon, you both head back to the hotel in a taxi.

You tell Zack Wonder all about your adventure. He's delighted, but he can see you're worn out from all that running. "Get some sleep," he says. "Big day tomorrow."

The next day, you get ready to head down to the dig with Guy Dangerous and the crew, while Karma Lee stays behind to do some interviews. "Good luck!" she says, with a wink and a wave . . .

Head to page 52.

You're standing in a dark, cobwebby museum storeroom. It's filled with a big mummy case, crates and statues, wrapped up in colorful cloths. There's nobody else around.

You can't tell where Montana has gone. He must be hiding . . . but where?

To fling open the mummy case, go to page 35.

To look into the crates, go to page 37.

To peer behind the statues, go to page 40.

You're getting nowhere. "I need to catch that guy!" you yell. You shove past the butler and run across the marble floor. Wow, this house is *glitzy*. Everything's polished to a shine.

The next moment, you're skidding across the floor on a loose rug. *Whoops!* That's the problem with polished floors. They're really slippery! Your feet flip out from under you and you take a tumble.

The butler looms over you. You can see right up his nose. "I'm calling the police!" he roars, pinning you down. You struggle to get away, but he's pretty strong for a skinny butler. Carrying trays full of cucumber sandwiches all day must build up a guy's muscles.

You end up being bound with tape and shoved into an empty mummy case, just in case you had any ideas about escaping. The bad news is that you're arrested for trespassing; the good news is you get a really hands-on experience of what it might have been like to be a pharaoh.

RUN AGAIN? TURN TO PAGE **4**

You open the mummy case. You see a hideous, twisted figure inside. It's not Montana Smith, it's just some long-dead dude.

Wow, being mummified doesn't improve your looks. This guy probably thought he was going to be preserved forever, just as handsome as he was when he was alive. Now he looks like a dried-up prune with teeth.

You close the case again, glad that you don't have to look at that creepy dead guy anymore. You need to keep searching for Montana.

To go look inside the crates, go to page 37.

To peer behind the statues, go to page 40.

You carefully put the plank down across the gap between the two buildings and walk out over it. On the next roof over, Montana is already pulling open a skylight and dropping down into the building. He's got a head start on you, but you think you can still catch him. And then, when you're halfway across, the plank breaks in half. *Whee!*

You have time to blink before you plummet into the dusty street below. Fortunately, a pile of crates breaks your fall. *Unfortunately*, the falls breaks a few of your bones. You end up in the hospital. You are covered from head to toe in bandages and groan a lot. If that wasn't bad enough, Guy Dangerous keeps making "curse of the mummy" jokes. What a guy!

RUN AGAIN? TURN TO PAGE **4**

You lift up the lid on one of the crates. There's nothing in here but dead beetles and some little carved models. You take a better look at those. There's a wooden ship, a chair, and something called a *shabti*, like a small doll. The Egyptians believed they could take these things with them into the afterlife. Fascinating stuff, but you're not here to learn. You're here to catch a thief.

To fling open the mummy case, go to page 35.

To peer behind the statues, go to page 40.

The trail leads you out into the desert, away from town. Soon there's not another person in sight. You walk over sand dunes that look silver in the moonlight. It's amazing to think that only a day or two ago, you were safe at home. Now you're hunting for a golden idol, alone, in the middle of the night, wearing an ancient mask. You don't know if this is the coolest thing you've ever done—or the craziest!

You follow the trail down into an open pit. You see a little pyramid down there. It's obviously been dug out recently. Your heart beats faster as you realize that this is the tomb Guy and you were supposed to explore tomorrow.

There are no security guards on patrol. Nobody sees you as you break the seal on the tomb door and slip inside. The mask on your face feels warm, as if it is coming to life.

You flick on your flashlight and gasp at the wonders you see inside the tomb. Wall paintings, grave goods, mummy cases . . . and stairs leading down. That's where the trail leads, so that's where you go.

Eventually, the mask guides you to a secret temple right in the heart of the tomb. You leave the heavy mask behind for now, and take a look around.

Turn to page 114.

Y ou walk over to poke behind the statues, most of which are draped in colorful cloth.

At first you see nothing unusual (well, other than ancient statues of animal-headed gods, which is pretty cool in itself). Then you notice one of the cloth-draped statues is a bit smaller than the others. And it's breathing.

You whip the fabric away to reveal Montana Smith.

"Aw, nuts!" he yells. "You just don't know when to quit, do you, kid?"

"Guess not," you say. "Drop that mask!"

He doesn't drop the mask. He shoves past you and dashes down the stairs, toward the main floor of the museum. You roll your eyes and sprint after him.

Head to page 42.

You heroically smash your way through the wooden door—and barge straight into a small child's birthday celebration, tipping over a huge table laden with delicious party food.

Montana isn't in here. Everyone inside was shouting because they're having fun.

They're not having fun anymore. The child's parents are furious. Men and women shake their fists at you and shout in Egyptian Arabic.

"Let me try something," Karma says. She starts dancing, spinning around and doing amazing high kicks. The children think she's wonderful, and clap and cheer. Unfortunately, the parents are not impressed.

The police pile in and you spend the next day in a cell, gloomily wishing you could be there for the tomb opening. End of the line!

RUN AGAIN? TURN TO PAGE **4**

Montana runs down the stairs. You tear after him. You burst through some double doors onto the main floor of the museum. It's small and quiet, but there are lots of cool objects on display and a replica war chariot in the middle of the room. Maybe you can come back for a real visit after the dig.

Montana's almost at the main door. If he gets out, he'll lose himself among the crowds in the street and you'll never catch him. You sprint like you've never sprinted before.

"See ya, loser!" Montana yells over his shoulder.

But he doesn't see Karma Lee run in from the street. She neatly kicks his feet out from under him with a single blow.

Montana yells and falls. He lets go of the mask, which goes sailing through the air toward a glass display case. You leap up after it and snatch it out of the air. *Phew!*

In one swift move, Karma slams the main door, locks it, and then holds Montana down with her knee. "I've heard some bad stuff about you, Smith, but I never had you pegged for a thief," she says.

"I ain't no thief!" Montana shouts angrily. He thrashes around, but Karma's got him pinned.

"Tell it to the cops," Karma sneers.

"I'll tell you if you give me a chance!" Montana mutters. "Just let me get a word in edgewise."

From the gathering noise outside, it sounds like there's an angry crowd wanting to get their hands on Montana. You guess your chase through the streets must have attracted a lot of attention. Clearly *they* all think he's a thief, too.

Someone bangs on the door. You could let them in, but you want to let Montana say his piece.

"You grabbed that mask and didn't pay for it," you tell him. "In my book, that makes you a thief."

"The mask was already stolen!" Montana yells. "It's called the Face of the Idol. That market trader guy must have lifted it from the dig you folks are here to film. It belongs in a museum."

"Yeah, right," says Karma. "You'd say *anything*."

"I'm serious!" Montana gurgles. Karma lets him breathe. "The trader's a tomb robber," Montana gasps. "I couldn't let him sell stolen artifacts for a fast buck."

Something doesn't add up. "So if you were doing the right thing," you ask, "why'd you keep running?"

"Because you were chasing me!" Montana yells. "Now I've got half of Egypt after me. So I need *you* to keep this mask safe, because I'm all out of ideas."

This is a tough call. You could look after the mask yourself, send the crowd the wrong way, and let Montana escape. It would be risky, especially if you were caught with the mask. On the other hand, maybe *Montana* should take all the risks. You could try to delay the crowd and let him go with the mask.

To take charge of the mask and let Montana escape, head to page 47.

To let Montana try to run away with the mask while you delay the crowd, head to page 49.

You find Zack in his hotel room. "Check this out!" he says, pointing at the TV.

Montana's run through the town with the stolen mask is all over the news! Your own TV cameras recorded quite a lot of the chase. Zack is glad you've got the mask safe and sound, and makes sure it gets passed on to the Egyptian authorities.

Unfortunately, those same authorities decide to cancel the tomb opening at the last minute. They don't want to let it go ahead until the security is up to standard—which it can't be, if people have been stealing from the dig site already.

Zack decides to take everyone to Cairo, so your vacation isn't a total bust. You enjoy a beautiful evening taking in the last existing wonder of the Seven Wonders of the World, the Great Sphinx of Giza, with your cohosts and friends.

"Look at that face," says Karma Lee, glancing up at the Sphinx. "I love how she looks. Like she's got thousands of years' worth of secrets, but she won't tell them to anyone."

You see what she means. It's as if the Sphinx is smiling down at you, about to whisper something incredible, but you won't ever get to hear it.

You're supposed to head home the next day. But you can't help wondering about all the mysteries you've learned of in the short time you've been here. What was that mask for? Where did it lead? And what wonders might have been lurking inside the tomb, waiting for you to find them?

RUN AGAIN? TURN TO PAGE 4

"We'll look after the mask," you say to Montana. "You get out of here."

Montana dusts himself off and passes you the mask. "Thanks for the vote of confidence, kid."

The angry crowd outside is getting louder.

"Get out of here!" Karma tells him. "Use the rooftops. They won't look for you there."

Montana turns to run back upstairs, then pauses. "You know, I never got the chance to try that thing on. But I kept getting the funny feeling I should. It's supposed to lead people to a priceless golden idol, did you know that?"

With a grin and a wave, Montana Smith is gone. Now you and Karma are stuck in an empty museum with a furious crowd outside and a possibly magical golden mask in your hands.

"Well," says Karma, "now what?"

"Maybe there's another way out?" you suggest.

The two of you run through to the rear of the building, where you find a door to a backstreet.

"I'll lead the crowd off this way," says Karma.

"Wait till the coast is clear, then get back to the hotel. OK?"

You nod. "Good luck!"

Karma leads the angry crowd on a wild goose chase while you quietly sneak away. You keep the mask hidden under your jacket. You know Zack will make sure it's returned to the proper authorities.

But once you're back in the safety of your hotel room, you can't resist trying the mask on. Amazingly, you can see a glowing golden thread leading out into the desert dunes. The mask is leading you to the idol, just like Montana said it would!

You could follow the trail out into the desert, all the way to wherever the idol is hidden. It would be dangerous, but unbelievably cool.

On the other hand, the mask is stolen, and probably should be put in safekeeping . . .

To follow the trail, head to page 38.

To find Zack Wonder so you can give him the mask, go to page 45.

You try to delay the crowd, but they're shoving their way in like shoppers on the first day of a post-Thanksgiving sale. "There's too many of them!" you yell to Karma.

The crowd piles in, knocking you aside. They catch Montana, who is led away in handcuffs, shouting that they've made a big mistake. He yells something about "the demon monkeys." You shake your head. Good thing you didn't believe him— what a weirdo.

"The heat must have gotten to him," Karma sighs.

You wonder why Montana would be raving about demon monkeys. As far as you know, there's nothing like that in Egyptian myth.

You're worn out from all that running, and that night you sleep deeply. The next day, everyone's buzzing with excitement as you get ready for the grand tomb opening. You and Guy have a delicious hotel breakfast of fresh fruit, toast, and juice, and chat about the crazy time you had yesterday in the market.

"Demon monkeys, huh?" Guy says, rubbing

his chin. "Like on that South American pyramid. I wonder . . ."

"What?" you ask.

"Oh, nothing," he says quickly. "Just a legend I heard. Silly stuff."

Karma stays behind to record some interviews with local archaeologists and other experts, while you head off to the tomb.

Head to page 52.

"Excuse me . . . pardon me . . . sorry!"

You barge through the crowd of tourists, trying as hard as you can not to step on anyone. Unfortunately, you step on quite a lot of people and knock one large gentleman into the pool. He flounders around, shouting at you in German.

"There she goes," Zack roars. "Get after her!"

You glance behind you at the chaos in your wake. Lots of tourists are glaring at you angrily and shaking their fists. Some of them are calling on their cell phones, probably to call security. You give them a last wave and shout, "Sorry!" but it doesn't seem to do any good.

Up ahead, Scarlett glares at you and dives through a doorway. You follow.

Head to page 113.

Y ou, Guy, Zack, and the film crew pile into a big SUV. You head out to the recently uncovered tomb, which lies several miles outside of town.

Guy can't sit still, he's so excited. "Nobody's been inside this tomb since it was sealed up thousands of years ago," he tells you. "Just think!"

"We *hope* nobody's been inside," Zack cuts in. "What if those relic robbers have managed to snoop around, Guy?"

Guy gives him an I-know-something-you-don't-know smile. "I know I made a big thing of it back at the hotel, but actually, you'd have to be one brave little robber to rob *this* tomb."

"Why?" you ask, curious.

"Because of the *curse*," Guy says, wiggling his fingers.

Zack chuckles and shakes his head. "A curse on an ancient Egyptian tomb? Sorry, man, but that's not the most original notion in the world."

"I know, right?" Guy laughs. "But there really is supposed to be a curse. Or there will be, once the seal is broken. That's what the inscriptions say."

"What seal?" you ask him.

"Easier if I just show you," says Guy with a wink. "Hey, did I ever tell you how mummies are made?"

For the rest of the journey, Guy goes into some pretty gross detail about ancient Egyptian embalming. When he gets to the part about how the embalmers pulled the corpse's brain out through the nose, Duke, the sound guy, turns green and has to open a window. You hope he doesn't puke.

"We're here!" shouts your driver suddenly.

Everyone piles out of the SUV and you get your first look at the tomb. You're standing at the edge of a crater in the sand, where the archaeologists have been digging. Down in the hole, you can see what looks like a small pyramid, about the size of a bus shelter, with inscriptions up the sides. Now that you're here, it actually feels kind of disappointing.

"You OK?" Guy asks.

"Sure," you tell him, hoping you don't look too ungrateful.

Guy instantly guesses what you're thinking. "Doesn't look like much, does it? Well, don't judge by appearances, that's all I'm saying." He winks again.

"I was expecting it to be a little bigger," you admit. You don't tell him that this tomb looks about as grand and interesting as your bedroom closet!

"This might just be the very top of it," Zack explains. "The archaeologists think there might be more underground."

Ah. That makes sense. You look again at the little pyramid sticking up out of the sand, and wonder if those sloping sides keep going where you can't see them. "How much more?"

"Maybe one or two chambers," Zack says with a shrug. "I guess we'll see. Or *you* will. You and Guy are going inside. I'm not."

"How come?"

Zack shudders. "I'm not crazy about small, cramped spaces."

"Hey!" Guy Dangerous calls from outside the tomb door. "You're going to want to see this!"

You half run, half slide down the sides of the crater and join him. Guy shows you a twisted rope across the front of the tomb door, tying the two bronze door handles together. A football-sized lump of wax covers up the knot in the rope, with some hieroglyphics pressed into it.

"That's the seal I told you about," he whispers. He runs a finger over it gently. "The tomb builders thought they were putting a curse on whoever opened this tomb. They didn't want anyone getting in."

You take a look at one of the inscriptions. It shows a hulking, monkey-like beast with a skull for a head. It's like nothing you've ever seen before, and it gives you a creepy feeling. All of a sudden, you wonder if the seal was put there to keep tomb robbers out . . . or to keep something else in.

Over the next hour, the film crew sets up cameras around the tomb entrance, ready to record the moment of truth when you go inside.

Zack takes you off for a quiet word. "You know, kid, I never really asked if *you* were OK with small, enclosed spaces. My bad. You don't have to go inside if you don't want to. There's going to be plenty to see and do out here."

"I'll think about it," you tell him. Zack pats you on the shoulder and leaves you to ponder.

Not long after that, Guy yells, "It's time! Let's get those cameras rolling. We're going to break the seal and go inside. Maybe our star presenter could cut the rope?"

You need to decide what to do. Guy is eager to

get inside the tomb, and you could break the seal and go with him like he's urging you to. You think there are probably some amazing sights to see inside.

But Zack said you didn't have to. You could stay outside and help operate the cameras. Guy will be disappointed, but it's your choice. Ancient tombs can be dangerous, and being trapped inside a musty chamber isn't your idea of a good way to die. You aren't sure about breaking that seal, either.

All that talk about ancient curses is probably ridiculous, but do you really want to take the risk?

If you want to join Guy, break the seal and head inside the tomb, then run to page 60.

If you'd rather stay outside with Zack and the rest of the crew and film the grand tomb opening with them, adding some commentary of your own, head for page 64.

You trudge across the dunes, gasping with thirst, eager to reach the cool water. But when you reach the spot, you find nothing there but smooth, dry sand.

Unfortunately, the shimmering pool was only an illusion caused by rising heat—a desert mirage. You are hardly the first person to be tricked by this. There are dozens of stories of hapless travelers wandering off into the sands, thinking there was water there.

Your head's spinning. You know there's only sand here, but that doesn't seem fair. You want to dive into water. Lovely, cool, refreshing water . . .

★

Some time later, Guy Dangerous and the crew drive up in their SUV.

"Found you!" Guy shouts triumphantly. "We've been looking all over for . . . um, kid? What are you doing?"

"Sploosh!" you shout crazily as you wave your arms and legs in the sand. "Check out my swimming pool!"

"I think your brains may have gotten a little cooked," Guy says.

"Splishy splashy," you giggle as Guy lifts you up gently and carries you to the SUV.

Zack Wonder takes care of you, giving you water to drink and putting a damp towel on your head, while Guy drives you to the nearest hospital. You soon recover, but you have to miss the filming.

You're alive, but you're a little embarrassed when Guy tells you what you had done. Don't worry, we won't tell anyone!

RUN AGAIN? TURN TO PAGE **4**

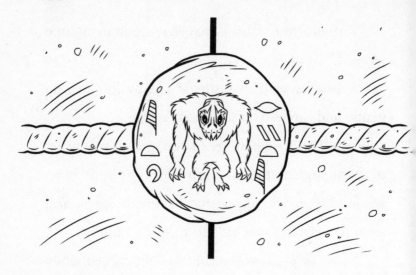

"OK, let's do this," you tell Guy.

He solemnly hands you his own personal machete. "One good chop should do it."

"Cameras are rolling!" yells Steve, the cameraman.

"Break a leg, everyone," says Zack. "Cut the rope, kid. Let's see what's in there."

You take a deep breath, swing the machete, and slice through the twisted rope. Your heart is beating like a wild drum solo. You half expect something strange to happen, but nothing really does.

There's a distant whooshing sound, but it's probably just the wind over the desert.

You and Guy grab one handle each and pull. The doors open with a slow, grinding groan, like a giant skeleton yawning awake after a long sleep. A waft of air, trapped for thousands of years, drifts into your nose. You smell something spicy and sweet, as well as a nasty smell of decay.

Guy shines his flashlight inside and lights up a small, stone-walled room. You hear him gasp.

There are paintings inside the tomb, as bright and fresh as the day they were drawn. Gods in thrones, with the heads of beetles and hawks, armies of men firing arrows at enemies, crocodiles swimming in rivers, big wiggly serpents, some important-looking dude in a chariot waving a flat hand at the sun . . .

You swallow hard and step inside. That sound of wind in the distance is getting louder. Then you see something incredible. Something that confirms what Zack told you before . . .

Stairs.

"Look!" you say to Guy, awed.

"Wow," says Guy. He shines his flashlight into

the dark corner and reveals the flight of stone steps. They go down, down, down under the desert, much farther than the archaeologists suspected.

"How deep does it go?" you ask in a hushed whisper.

"Only one way to find out." Guy grins. "Want to explore?"

"Do I!"

You and Guy climb down the steps into the musty interior of the tomb and explore its silent passages. This place is fascinating, with chambers and hallways and stairways leading from one level to the next. It's never-ending.

At some point, you notice that the crew isn't behind you anymore. Maybe they've wandered off to take some establishing shots. You don't give it much thought, though: you're too excited by the stunning discovery that the tomb is only the very tip of a colossal unknown pyramid buried beneath the desert sands.

"We need to explore as much of this place as we

can," Guy says happily. "In fact, we could split up if you like. I don't want to hold you back. Just don't break anything."

You can choose what you'd like to do. Guy's about to move off down a long corridor. You could go with him if you want to.

However, Guy does keep hurrying on to the next chamber before you can have a good look around. He's just that excited! If you hang back a bit and let him go on ahead, you could slow down and have a really close look around inside the tomb chambers.

To go with Guy down the long corridor, head to page 67.

To explore inside one of the chambers yourself, go to page 68.

"Y ou're not coming in?" Guy says, surprised. "Are you sure?"

"The sun and the sand feel great out here," you laugh. "You go on ahead."

"Okey-dokey, then!" Guy cracks his knuckles, pulls out his machete, and hacks through the rope holding the door shut. The wax seal falls to the ground and cracks in two. Guy pulls open the tomb doors, flicks on his flashlight and heads inside.

The moment the tomb is unsealed, a strange rushing sound begins in the distance and grows louder by the minute. The crew looks at one another anxiously. *What was that about a curse?* you think.

Zack Wonder runs to the top of a sand dune, shades his eyes, and peers out across the desert. "Sandstorm!" he yells. "Get to cover! Protect the cameras! MOVE!"

"What about Guy?" you yell.

"He'll be fine—he's in shelter already. We're the ones in danger!"

Maybe you should have headed into the tomb

when you had the chance. You start running down into the crater, but the next moment, a blinding spray of sand rushes up all around you. You're surrounded by stinging, dusty clouds, and you can't see a thing.

"Zack!" you yell, but all you hear back is a faint cry. You cover your eyes and run, heading for the SUV—or, at least, for where you remember it being parked. Sand gets into your mouth and makes your tongue gritty. You try opening your eyes for a second, but the sandstorm forces you to close them again.

You run and run, soft sand sliding under your feet. You lose all track of time. After minutes, or hours—you can't tell—the storm starts to die down. Your arms sting a little from the sand, but apart from that, you're fine.

As the clouds begin to clear, you realize you've become separated from the crew. Somehow you've managed to wander, disorientated, into the desert. It's as if a supernatural force is playing tricks on you.

At least I've got some water, you think to yourself.

Besides, the film crew can't be too far away, can they?

You couldn't have run all that far . . .

You trudge across the sand, moving from one dune to the next. Time passes. You see nobody. It's as if you've been snatched up and taken to some endless desert out of the Arabian Nights.

After many hours of wandering, carefully rationing your water, you finally see some landmarks. To one side you think you can make out a trail, as if a group of animals had passed by. To the other, you see the shimmer of water—possibly an oasis.

To head to the trail, ǥo to paǥe 70.

To make for the ǥleaminǥ water, ǥo to paǥe 58.

Y ou and Guy head down the colorful corridor, marveling at the images of gods and pharaohs on the walls. You still wish he'd slow down a little so you could spend more time looking at the sights, but he's just too excited.

Halfway along, Guy finds a statue of a hawk on a pedestal. "I never could resist grabbing idols," he jokes, and picks it up.

To your horror, the pedestal moves. It's a trap! You hear sliding sand, and then a stone wall begins to move across the corridor, closing you off from the way back to the surface.

Guy can't possibly get through in time, but you can. Do you dive through the narrowing gap while you have a chance, or stick with Guy even though you might both be trapped?

To jump through the gap, head to page 75.

To stick with Guy, head to page 72.

"Y ou go on ahead," you tell Guy. "I'm going to have a look around."

"Sure!" Guy yells back to you. You hear him whistling as he wanders off through the labyrinth.

The room you're in is stacked high with burial goods. There's a long, stretched-out figure of a sleek black dog in the middle.

You recognize him—that's the tomb guardian Anubis, who sometimes appears as a man with a dog's head, and sometimes just as a dog. Against the wall is a chair made of gilded wood. You let your gaze rove over dozens of jars with animal head–shaped stoppers, and wonder what might be inside. Mummified human organs, probably. You're awestruck. Everything around you is so . . . old.

Anubis seems to be looking at you, as if to ask what you're doing here. "Good dog," you tell him. You get the silly idea to pat his head, so you do.

Click. Slowly, a panel swings open in the base of the Anubis statue. You shine your flashlight inside. Against all odds, you've found a secret door on your very first trip into the tomb chambers!

It opens up to a shaft below, where handholds have been cut into the stone, forming a primitive ladder. You think you glimpse a sarcophagus gleaming in the darkness. Something about the way it's arranged gives you the feeling that it's a very sacred place— perhaps even a temple. You could easily climb down. But do you want to? You could always go and rejoin Guy Dangerous.

To run and rejoin Guy, head to page 67.

To climb down the shaft, head to page 114.

Fortunately, the trail was real and not a mirage. It's not long before a line of people riding on camels comes trotting along. They take one look at you and lift you up on to a camel's back, so they can give you a ride back to town.

"People still ride camels in Egypt?" you mumble.

One of the riders grins at you. "We're tourists!" she says. "I'm Wendy and this is Otis. Abdullah here is giving us an authentic camel train experience. Isn't it romantic?"

"It's making my rump sore," grumbles a man who is probably her husband. "And I got sand in my—"

"Isn't it lucky we found you out here?" Wendy interrupts. "What on earth were you doing out in the desert on your own, anyway?"

"Exploring an ancient tomb," you tell them. "With a curse on it."

Wendy laughs loudly. "Oh, that's funny! A cursed tomb! You should be on television, honey. You're a natural comedian."

"I was supposed to be on television," you mutter,

but fortunately she doesn't hear you.

Together, you make your weary way back to town. Abdullah, the guide, quietly tells you, "I know you are telling the truth. But I think it is better that you did not go inside that place. People who have spent time there at night have heard roars, like some great wild beast."

"From near the tomb?"

"From inside the tomb," he says. And that's all he has to say on the subject.

Your first experience of broadcasting has been a disaster, but at least you survived. You can't help wondering what was in that tomb, though, curse or no curse.

There's one way to find out . . .

RUN AGAIN? TURN TO PAGE **4**

The stone slab grinds across the corridor. It seals you in, separating you from the route back up to the surface.

Guy puffs out his cheeks. "OK. I guess we're not exploring anymore. What we need to do now is escape!"

You run down to the other end of the corridor, but to your dismay it's a dead end. "I think we're trapped," you tell him.

Guy pulls out his phone and tries to call Zack, but you're so far underground that there's no signal at all. "Great," he says. "So much for that idea . . ."

"We're going to get through this," you tell him, sounding as brave as you can. "We just have to put our heads together and come up with a plan."

"That's right. We'll think of something." Guy gives you a fist bump. "There's got to be a way out."

You sit down and think hard, trying to pinpoint anything that might be a clue. Guy does the same. The minutes tick past. A scarab beetle scuttles over your knuckles.

"Hey!" you say, jumping to your feet. "Remember how we heard sand when you triggered the trap?"

"Yeah, so?"

"So we didn't see any. There must be some sort of mechanism behind the walls. That means there are other rooms in here . . ."

You bang on the wall until you find a hollow area. You and Guy grin at each other. Secret passage!

Together you pry the plaster off the wall, revealing sandstone blocks. It doesn't take long to pull one of them out. You and Guy wriggle through into a new corridor.

Guy whistles softly. "Nice work, kid. Look at the size of this place."

You've broken through into a whole new part of the tomb!

Guy steps forward and a slab underfoot goes *click*. *Whoops* . . . Guy just isn't having much luck with the traps, it seems!

There's a crashing sound behind you, and sand comes pouring in through the split-open ceiling.

You and Guy sprint down the hieroglyph-lined corridor, with a tidal wave of sand coming after you. In the confusion, Guy drops his flashlight.

You can see it shining on the floor. It's about to be buried under the flood of sand. You could dive back for it and risk being buried yourself, or run blindly forward into the darkness.

To dive back for the flashlight, head to page 80.

To keep running into the darkness ahead, dash to page 77.

You dive through the narrowing gap with seconds to spare.

You can hear Guy yelling from the other side of the wall: "Get help! I can't see any way out—I'm trapped! HELP!"

The adventure has taken a sudden turn for the worse! You think about running up to get the rest of the film crew, but figure that would take too long. You decide to rescue Guy yourself.

You shine your flashlight around the corridor you're in. Along its length are statues of the Egyptian gods in little alcoves. You pick one of them up. It's heavy, like a club. That gives you an idea. The slab that closed off the corridor wasn't very thick. You think you could break it.

Heroically, you wallop the slab with the statue. The slab doesn't break, but the statue smashes to pieces. You think a few more blows is all it will take, though. Fortunately, there are more statues here . . .

You smash some more statues against the slab. Guy keeps yelling, which is a good sign. It means he's still alive in there. But you don't manage to break the slab, or even crack it.

Eventually, a rescue team arrives. They send you back up to the surface.

Unfortunately, you are in deep trouble with the Egyptian authorities, who are less than pleased about the damage done to their statues. While the rescue team opens up the slab with their equipment, you are sent home in disgrace. Needless to say, you don't get to make a TV show with Zack Wonder. But you do get a reputation for breaking things!

RUN AGAIN? TURN TO PAGE 4

Y ou and Guy run along the corridor in total
darkness. Any moment now, you expect to trip
over a loose stone or a mummy's leg or something,
but luckily you don't. You keep running until the
sound of flowing sand stops.

"You still there?" asks Guy's voice, somewhere
close to you.

"Yeah," you answer. "Wish I'd brought a flashlight,
too."

"You and me both. Hold on, don't panic. I've got
an idea."

Guy lights a match from a book of matches he
picked up back at the hotel. The flame illuminates
his stubbly face like a Halloween mask.

You get a shock when you see what you've run
into. All around you are mummies lying on dusty
pallets. You're not that scared—they're just dead
folks, they can't hurt you—but you do wish there
was a bit more light in here.

"Perfect!" Guy says. To your disgust, he rigs a

burning torch out of bits of a resinous rag peeled off a nearby mummy.

"Nobles burn better than commoners," he quips.

You work your way down the corridor by the light of the mummy-torch and come to a junction.

To the left, you can smell strange herbal scents. "Those are embalming spices," Guy tells you. "There must be a lot more mummies that way."

To the right, you smell the scent of clean, fresh water running over rocks. An underground stream, maybe?

To head left toward the mummies, go to page 148.

To head right toward the water, go to page 81.

O ne moment you're staggering down a flight of stone steps, the next you're on your hands and knees in some sort of shrine.

A statue of an ibis-headed god looms over you, holding up an ankh, the Egyptian symbol of life. Behind you, you hear the demon monkey come crashing down the stairs.

There's only one exit from this room—a chain that dangles into a well-like shaft in the corner. You think you could climb down it, but you'd have to move fast to escape the monkey.

Or maybe you should take a few precious seconds to try to block the entrance instead, to slow the monkey and give you more time? That statue could do the job.

To start climbing down the chain right away, turn to page 152.

To try to block the entrance with that god statue, turn to page 151.

You grab the flashlight, but the rolling wave of sand knocks you off your feet. The next second, it's buried you completely.

You have a few moments to think about how you used to really like sand. It was great when you were making sand castles out of it or running across it beside the sea. Tombs full of sand, however, are just not so much fun.

RUN AGAIN? TURN TO PAGE **4**

You stumble into an underground shrine. There's a statue against the wall of a god with a crook in one hand and a grain flail in the other. At his feet is a trough painted with wheat, as if the god was making the crops grow.

"Osiris," says Guy. "God of the afterlife and the underworld, as well as the fertile land. Important fellow."

You look around to find where the sound of running water is coming from. The shrine is built around a natural spring in one of the walls, where a trickle of fresh water comes bubbling from the rocks and vanishes into the ground again.

"Water in the desert must have been important, too," you guess.

Guy nods. "This was probably the foundation spot for the whole tomb."

It's not very impressive—just a feeble little stream—but the ancient Egyptians must have thought it was sacred.

The spring is dropping slowly into a pottery cup.

The water looks drinkable, and you badly want to drink some to quench your thirst.

Or you could pour the water into the stone trough in front of Osiris, in case it triggers some sort of mechanism. This whole setup seems like a riddle of some kind, or maybe a test.

Whichever choice you make, bear in mind that the spring flows very slowly and will probably not fill the cup again for hours!

To drink the water, head to page 85.

To pour it into the stone trough, go to page 86.

By the flickering light of the mummy-torch, you walk slowly across the room. The monkey mummy—if that's what it is—sits bundled up in its bandages, not moving.

You come closer, and closer, until you're nearly looking it in the face. It's an ugly brute, all dry skin, loose bandages, and empty eye sockets. It was probably just as ugly when it was alive, thousands of years ago.

It couldn't have moved. It's obviously dead. But you're certain you saw it twitch.

Wait—did you just hear a noise? A sound of scraping, like claws on stone . . .

"Guy?" you whisper.

"I heard it, too," he says.

You lean in close, looking right at the mummy.

It twitches again. You jump back with a yell.

You half expect the mummy to lunge for you, but no. A huge rat pokes its head out of the mummy's middle, looks around, and vanishes inside it again. Gross, but not dangerous.

Behind you, Guy sighs in relief. "It's a rat. That's all. Just a rat."

Silly, you think to yourself. Whoever heard of mummified monkeys coming back to life?

You head back the other way.

Turn to page 81.

The water is fresh and delicious. You share it with Guy. But only moments afterward, you're thirsty again, as if the whole desert was drying up your throat. You scramble to catch the last drops.

Guy's torch burns out, but he doesn't bother to make a new one. He's desperate for the precious, sacred water, too. This is a bit embarrassing . . . The pair of you have earned the curse of Osiris! The more water you drink, the thirstier you become.

Eventually, a rescue team comes to free you. They find you and Guy slurping at the sacred spring, trying to lick water off the rock.

You spend the rest of your life drinking anything you can get your hands on, and nothing ever seems to quench your raging thirst. Fish no longer feel safe around you. Swimming pools are forced to close. Curses are serious business, you know!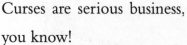

RUN AGAIN? TURN TO PAGE **4**

Y ou carry the full cup over to the trough by the painting of the wheat and tip it in.

"You sure you know what you're doing?" Guy says, scratching his head.

"I've got a hunch . . ."

"I hope so, because that was the only water we had."

The water trickles down slowly into a hidden compartment and triggers a mechanism. The statue of Osiris grinds around in a half-circle and reveals a way forward. Guy looks at you, impressed. "I'll trust your hunches from now on."

You and Guy excitedly climb through the new door into a wide chamber. To your right is a dead-end alcove where fresh-looking writing has been scrawled on the walls. To your left is a second shrine, this one with a statue of a dog-headed god, Anubis, holding a set of scales.

To go right into the alcove, turn to page 91.

To go left to the shrine, turn to page 93.

"Stop right there, Smith!" yells Karma.

The two of you run after him, into the dusty alley that smells of cumin and coriander.

Montana looks back and sees you coming. "*Nooo!*" he cries and puts on a burst of speed.

You and Karma Lee pursue Montana down the length of the alley. He dodges trash bins, nearly falls over a cat, and dives out into the street on the other side.

You hear him yell, "Taxi!"

Before you can catch up with him, he's flagged down a cab and flung himself onto the backseat. He clings tightly to the golden mask. The cab begins to move away.

"We're losing him!" Karma says. "What do we do?"

That's up to you.

You could run into the traffic, jump, and hang on to the back of Montana's cab. That's a pretty crazy move, but you wouldn't be giving up, right?

Or you could flag down your own cab and chase him. That could be safer, but it might take longer.

You glance around, looking for other options. Someone's left a bicycle outside a nearby shop. There's no lock. You and Karma could grab the bike and ride after Montana. You wouldn't be stealing it, just borrowing it for a while . . .

To grab on to the back of Montana's cab, go to page 13.

To hail your own cab, go to page 14.

To borrow the bicycle and chase after Montana on that, head to page 15.

You call Zack on the phone and explain what's happening. "I'll be right there!" he yells. "Don't even think about tackling Scarlett on your own!"

Only minutes later, a group of SUVs roars up to join you. They're full of Egyptian police officers, along with Zack Wonder, who slaps you on the back. "Good call," he says warmly. "You did the right thing."

Zack and the police officers hide in the cave, and the SUV drivers zoom off so that Scarlett won't see them and suspect anything. Now you just have to wait. You feel like the bait in a trap, and it's not a nice sensation.

Sure enough, the headlights of Scarlett's car appear. There's a squeal of brakes, and then Scarlett herself comes striding over the dunes toward you. "Let me see it!" she shouts. "Prove you weren't lying."

You hold up the golden idol.

Scarlett grins and runs up to you. One of the Egyptian policemen yells, and Scarlett is suddenly surrounded. Handcuffs are slapped on her. You back away as she's bundled into an SUV with tinted windows. "You double-crosser!" she shouts. "You rotten, cheating little . . . *ooh*! Playing both sides against the middle, eh? Who do you think you are? *Me?*"

She's whisked off for questioning, while the idol is taken to a museum.

Congratulations—you've thwarted a major crime and helped to make a blockbuster TV show, too. It's only a matter of time before the networks recognize your talent and sign you up for a major deal. Stardom awaits!

RUN AGAIN? TURN TO PAGE **4**

You look up at the hieroglyphic writing. It's fresh and wet—and glows faintly in the dark!

"Wait, this doesn't make sense," you say. "This looks like it was only done a few hours ago. But it's the same kind of writing that's all over this tomb."

"And that's thousands of years old," Guy says. He takes some pictures of the inscriptions on his phone. "I wonder what it says?"

You shudder. "Maybe it's best we don't know."

"Come on, where's your spirit of discovery?" Guy teases. "I've got my textbook right here. I can translate the writing easily. It might take a while, but we could learn something."

It's your call. Translate the weird writing, or keep moving and look for an exit?

To take the time to translate the inscription, go to page 94.

To keep moving out of the tomb, go to page 93.

The rest of the evening is much more fun. You zoom back to the hotel and watch your complimentary DVD of *Zack Wonder's 100 Greatest Sporting Moments* with commentary from the man himself!

In the morning, you learn that someone's already been inside the tomb overnight. You and Zack exchange glances. It's pretty clear who it was. The dig has to be canceled, as the site is no longer secure. Zack knows it's not your fault, and he'll hire you to host a different episode of *Wonders of the Universe* instead.

But you can't help wondering what was down there, waiting for you to discover it …

RUN AGAIN? TURN TO PAGE **4**

You look around for a way out of the Anubis shrine, but you don't see one. "This must be another test," you guess. "What do we know about this dude?"

"According to the legends, Anubis used to weigh the hearts of dead people in the afterlife," Guy whispers. "If you passed his test, you got through to paradise, or candy land, or wherever. If not . . ."

You notice that one of the scales Anubis is holding has a nasty dried-up object in it—hopefully not a real heart!—and the other is empty. "I think we should put something in the empty scale," you suggest.

"Good idea," Guy says. "Come and look at these."

He shows you some objects lying on a nearby altar: a rock, a bone, and a feather. "Maybe one of these should go in it," you guess.

Turn to page 96 to choose the rock.

Turn to page 97 to choose the bone.

Or turn to page 98 to choose the feather.

Guy gives you the mummy-torch to hold while he opens up his hieroglyphic textbook. "Let's see. Two little walking feet, eye, wavy lines . . ."

Guy reads the words out as he translates them. "I summon the *shabtis*, servants of Pharaoh, those who watch and wait in the world beyond."

You walk up and down and hum a tune as he translates. It makes you feel less creeped out.

Guy reads a bit about "the men who are not men," and how they must now "make us ready for the passage to the afterlife." Then he stops. "That's it. That's where it ends."

"Did that sound like a spell to you?"

"Yeah. Let's get out of here . . . whoa! Look!"

You look up and see that the writing has disappeared. Guy checks his phone. The photo shows only the bare wall. The writing's vanished from there, too.

"That can't be a great sign . . ." you say.

The next moment, little blue wax figures come marching into the room. As crazy and surprising as this is, you have to laugh, because they're small and stumpy and kind of cute, and move with a waddle. You and Guy have accidentally summoned the *shabtis*, who were meant to be the pharaoh's servants in the afterlife!

Unfortunately, they suddenly become a lot less cute when they start trying to mummify you. After all, what self-respecting pharaoh wouldn't want to be mummified? They begin to wrap you and Guy up in bandages. You just have to hope a rescue crew finds you before the *shabtis* start stuffing you with spices and salt!

RUN AGAIN? TURN TO PAGE **4**

Anubis is not pleased with your choice. A righteous person's heart should be as light as a feather, not as heavy as a rock!

The floor gives way beneath you, and you catch a glimpse of a gigantic beast moving in the darkness. "It's *Ammit!*" yells Guy. "The devourer of souls!"

You just have time to think how cool it would look if this were a movie. That monster is pretty wicked, you have to admit.

Too bad it's going to eat you. *Chomp!*

RUN AGAIN? TURN TO PAGE **4**

Nothing happens. The bone is clearly the wrong choice. You'd have thought a dog god like Anubis would go for a bone. Maybe he's more the squeaky-ball kind of god?

Now that you think about it, the bone might not have been part of the test. Maybe it was just the remains of an ancient pyramid builder's lunch.

"Better choose again," says Guy.

Go back to page 93 and try a different option.

You gently place the feather in the scale. Anubis is pleased with your choice. The heart of the sinless person is light.

With an ominous rumble, the whole statue sinks into the floor on a pillar of rock. There's a circular opening left where it once stood. You and Guy look at one another.

"Impressive," Guy says, giving a soft whistle. "That was one heck of a test. Whatever's down there must be pretty important."

You and Guy climb down and find yourselves in what looks like a burial chamber.

A stone sarcophagus sits in the middle of the room. To one side, an opening leads to a steep slope down into the dark. You can see a wall blocking it off partway down. Another dead end? You gulp, wondering if you're ever going to escape this tomb.

The flickering torch lights up piles and piles of wonderful things. You were right about the treasure.

You see golden figurines, pieces of jewelry inlaid with lapis lazuli, mystical amulets, bowls brimming over with gems, and beads of precious metal. It's so astounding, it takes your mind off being trapped.

"Is this the pharaoh's tomb?" you wonder.

"I don't think so," Guy says.

"But . . . look at all this stuff!" How could this not be a royal hoard?

"It's probably a false tomb, to fool tomb robbers," Guy says. "They left some treasure lying around to make thieves think they'd found the right place. The real tomb must still be in here somewhere, hidden away."

You stare again at the mounds of riches. "So if this is what's in the fake tomb, what's in the *real* one?"

"Something more valuable still," Guy says quietly.

Just then, the ancient mechanism that lowered the statue of Anubis breaks.

Stone counterweights come crashing through the ceiling. Dust fills the air. The whole area begins to cave in around you.

"It's collapsing!" Guy shouts. "We've got to get to safety!"

"But there's no way out!" you yell back.

You'll have to think of something fast. You could climb inside the sarcophagus to shelter from falling rocks and hope the cave-in stops. It does look pretty sturdy, and there would be room for you in there, as well as any mummies that happened to be lying around.

Or you could get Guy to shove the sarcophagus aside, in case there's a hidden exit underneath it.

To climb in the sarcophagus, head to page 102.

To shove the sarcophagus away with Guy's help, head to page 103.

You summon up every scrap of courage you've got and brace yourself to fight. The mummified demon monkey roars at you. Its breath smells horrible.

How are you going to fight? You could charge at the demon monkey, waving your fists and yelling, in the hope of scaring it off. It probably won't be expecting that.

Or you could try grabbing a weapon. You look around and notice a ceremonial sword sitting on a side altar. It's shaped a bit like a long sickle. It might not be much use after sitting in a tomb for thousands of years, though, and the warranty is definitely expired . . .

To wave your fists and yell, head to page 139.

To grab the ceremonial sword and swing it at the demon monkey, head to page 140.

You climb inside the sarcophagus and lie down alongside the bandaged remains of some ancient scribe or other. Guy has other ideas. He runs away down the slope, yelling your name.

Rocks pile down on top of the sarcophagus. You wait until the rattling and thumping has stopped, and then try to lift the lid. It won't budge.

Oops. You realize the pile of rocks on top of it is making it too heavy to remove . . . ever again.

Well, the bad news is you're buried alive in the middle of a pyramid. The good news? There isn't any. Oh, you're not alone, which is something—but the mummy lying next to you doesn't seem to feel like chatting. He's going to be pretty boring company for the next thousand years or so.

RUN AGAIN? TURN TO PAGE **4**

"Guy! Help me with this!"

Together, you shove the sarcophagus as hard as you can. Dust falls into your eyes, and rocks are crashing down around you.

"Heave!" you yell.

The sarcophagus is easier to move than you expected. From the noise it makes, it must be on stone rollers. But to your horror, there's no hidden staircase, no trapdoor, nothing.

"Kid, keep pushing!" Guy yells. "This thing is our ticket out of here!" You don't understand what he means, but you keep pushing anyway. You push and push until the sarcophagus tips over into the sloping passage. It goes rumbling down the slope, picking up speed as it goes. You suddenly realize it's going to smash straight through the wall of stone blocks!

You and Guy run after it, whooping like cowboys, while stony debris comes crashing down behind you.

The sarcophagus smashes through the wall and keeps going. A cool breeze blows from the other side. Fresh air? That means a way back to the surface!

Guy leaps up and lands on the sarcophagus, using it like a surfboard!

You could probably run, jump, and join him on the sarcophagus. But then, on the other side of the broken wall, you see a corridor leading back into the tomb. A strange, golden light glimmers at the far end.

What could possibly be reflecting back a golden light? Clearly, this tomb has more hidden mysteries. What was it Guy was saying about a "real tomb" somewhere inside?

Maybe you should run down the corridor and see what's casting that beautiful light. You won't have Guy with you, though. He's sarcophagus-surfing on out of here. And the corridor will probably cave in behind you. That's okay, right?

To run down the corridor toward the light, head to page 114.

To jump on the sarcophagus and surf out of the tomb with Guy, head to page 108.

You lower yourself into the pit and wait for Scarlett to show up. There's a scuttling noise. The sand around you begins to twitch.

Uh-oh. You realize, too late, that the many-legged creature is a scorpion. This was once the sacred shrine of Selket, the scorpion goddess, and it looks like some of her friends are still here! Zack yells a warning, but it's too late. Scorpions come pouring out of the sand and swarm up your legs. You find that they're surprisingly tickly—until they start biting.

Ouch! You get stung a *lot*, but luckily the hospital is really comfortable. Zack Wonder visits you every day, bringing you cards from well-wishers and fresh fruit from the market.

One of the cards you get is from Scarlett Fox. It just says "Sorry." Inside is a picture of her holding a golden idol and winking. What is *that* about?

RUN AGAIN? TURN TO PAGE **4**

You point out the mystery woman to Zack Wonder. The moment he sees her, he scowls. "You say she had some sort of scanner?"

"That's right. She was waving it around, trying not to be seen."

"I know who that is, kid. It's Scarlett Fox. She pretends to be an explorer, but she's really this hotshot British corporate super-spy. What is she doing in my hotel, snooping around?"

As if she'd overheard you, Scarlett Fox darts off toward the double doors that lead out of the dining hall.

"We'd better tail her," you tell him. "If she gets away, we'll never know what she was doing here."

Zack nods. "That girl never goes sniffing around unless there's something big in it for her. She's after something. We can be sure of that. And I bet it's tied with the big tomb opening tomorrow."

You and Zack sidle around the outside of the room, dodging out of the way of hotel guests and politely refusing offers of finger food from waiters.

You eventually reach the doors and slip through into the corridor.

You see Scarlett at the end of the hallway, holding her scanner device in front of a vase of flowers. She hasn't noticed you yet. You both shuffle along, keeping to the shadows, while Scarlett glances to the left and right before moving on.

"Listen, kid," Zack whispers to you, "sneaking around like this isn't exactly my style. Let me do it the way we do on the football field, OK?"

"And what would that look like?"

Zack flexes. "I'll chase her down."

It's up to you.

Do you go along with Zack's plan, break into a run, and charge Scarlett? Go to page 109.

Or do you keep it sneaky and sidle along quietly, keeping her in view? Go to page 121.

108

You and Guy ride the sarcophagus out of the smashed-open hole in the wall and land on the sandy floor of a cave. It's a natural rocky cavern, not part of the pyramid. That must mean you've escaped!

Then you notice an incredibly surprised film crew staring at you. They had gone down here to film some moody shots of empty caverns, and didn't expect their star host to come flying out of a hole using a sarcophagus as a surfboard.

The contents of the sarcophagus are fortunately not damaged. The camera pans over an ancient gold mask, jeweled scarabs, and gleaming rings, and a rather battered-looking mummy. What a find! Your tomb exploration is over, but you've had the adventure of a lifetime!

You do wonder about that "real tomb" Guy mentioned, though, and the priceless treasure you've been told is inside . . .

RUN AGAIN? TURN TO PAGE 4

"OK," you whisper, "on three. One, two ..."

Zack charges down the hotel corridor, right toward Scarlett. Just then, a door opens and a tired-looking maid pushes a cleaning cart into the hall. Zack can't stop. He crashes right through it.

Scarlett jumps several feet in the air at the noise, and then breaks into a run. Her red hair trails behind her like a banner.

"Stay where you are, Miss Fox!" bellows Zack. "You're in trouble!"

Scarlett doesn't reply. She vaults neatly over a cart laden with empty dinner plates. Zack just crashes right through that, too, knocking it over.

You run after them both, your heart pounding as you struggle to keep up. You can't help but feel a bit pleased that you were right about her being up to no good—she wouldn't be running if she hadn't done something wrong!

Scarlett clatters down some steps. You see a sign, in English and Arabic, that reads SWIMMING POOL. You and Zack follow her down there. She flings the doors open and runs, gasping, along the sunny edge of the pool. There are crowds of tourists sitting and lying there, their towels spread out. Scarlett leaps over all of them as if they're merely hurdles.

Which way do you run? You could chase Scarlett down the sunny side of the pool, but it might mean having to dodge and knock tourists out of the way. Or you could run around to the far, shady side, which is empty. It's less direct, but you wouldn't have to barge through any crowds. Which would be quicker?

To take the crowded way, football style, turn to page 51.

To take the longer, easier route, go to page 112.

"Stairs!" you shout to Zack. You charge through the door and start to take the steps at a run. The bad news is that there are dozens of flights. This is the main hotel staircase. You quickly see why most people take the elevator.

But the good news is that you chose right. Scarlett's running up the stairs! You know it's her because you hear her muttering in a crisp British accent, only a few flights ahead of you.

You race up and up and up until you are gasping for breath. The next moment you've burst out on to the hotel roof. Nowhere for Scarlett to run now!

Head to page 127.

Y ou run around to the far side of the pool.
Zack goes with you. By the time you make it
all the way around, there's no sign of Scarlett.

"She gave us the slip," sighs Zack.

"We should have run through that crowd of
tourists," you mutter gloomily to yourself. "Then we
would've caught her."

"Ah, don't beat yourself up!" Zack grins. "You
didn't want to cause a ruckus, and I can respect that.
That's a gold star near your name in Zack Wonder's
book."

His kind words make you feel a bit better. With
Scarlett out of sight, there's nothing to do but to go
back to your room and watch movies on cable TV
until it's time for the dig.

Head to page 52.

You burst into the corridor, run around two sharp bends, and emerge into a plush hallway just in time to see the elevator doors closing in front of you.

At the same time, you hear the sound of a door nearby banging shut. But you can't tell whether it was the door to the hotel kitchens, which are a little way ahead, or the door to the stairs.

"Where'd she go?" Zack asks, confused.

What do you think? The elevator doors are almost closed, but Zack could probably pull them open. It would be quicker to check one of the doors, though.

If you run through the door to the stairs, dash to page 111.

If you barge through to the kitchens, run to page 116.

If you get Zack to pull the elevator doors open with his powerful grip, zoom to page 118.

Deep inside the hidden tomb, you find yourself in the king's burial chamber temple.

You're so excited, you almost forget to breathe. You're in a secret treasure house that no mortal has set eyes on for thousands of years.

The unknown pharaoh is inside a golden coffin in the center of the room. He would have believed in life after death, of course, and so he was buried with all the jewels and household items he thought he would need to be comfortable in the next life. There's even model food made from wood.

There, on a pedestal, sits a strange golden idol. It doesn't look Egyptian—in fact, it looks more like an Aztec or Inca relic. It's shaped like a scowling dude gripping his legs. Can it be . . . solid gold? It must be worth millions if it is. Not to mention its value to archaeology!

Your fingers tingle. As you move toward the idol, the whole room begins to shake. Dust falls from the ceiling. It feels like the temple is going to collapse!

On instinct, you pick up the idol to stop it from

being lost forever in the cave-in. But the moment you touch it, a roar erupts in the chamber.

A terrifying creature crashes through a wall. It looks like a gigantic monkey covered with mummy wrappings. Instead of a head, it has only a huge, blackened-looking skull. Bandages trail from its huge arms, which end in outstretched claws. It's coming for you!

Do you fight, on page 101?

Or do you flee, on page 144?

You crash into the kitchens just as a heavily laden waiter is coming the other way, carrying a huge pyramid of falafels on a silver tray. Everything seems to go in slow motion. Terror fills the waiter's face as you collide with him. He flings his arms up. The tray soars into the air. Falafels fly across the room like little meteors.

The waiter staggers backward and crashes into a chef. The chef loses his grip on the pot he was carrying, showering everyone in expensive, spicy soup. Meanwhile, Zack Wonder comes charging into the kitchen behind you. He skids on a falafel, slams into your back, and sends you shooting through the air.

For three seconds, you fly like a superhero. Then you land in the middle of a wedding banquet that the hotel was preparing. Your face plunges deep into a cake. It's delicious, but quite a lot of it goes up your nose.

The kitchen staff quickly calls security. The manager of the hotel is furious. Zack only manages to smooth things over by agreeing to pay a lot of money. By the time everything's calmed down again, Scarlett Fox is long gone.

You have no choice but to head back to your room and take a shower. In the morning, while you're still picking bits of wedding cake out of your ears, you get some terrible news. The dig's been canceled, because someone has broken into the tomb overnight. You're pretty sure it was Scarlett Fox, though of course you can't prove it . . . and now it's time for you to head home.

RUN AGAIN? TURN TO PAGE **4**

*Z*ack wrenches the elevator doors open. This startles some tourists. "Is the elevator broken?" they ask, confused. "Have you come to let us out?"

"Scarlett's not in here," you say to Zack.

Zack groans. "We need to find her!" he says.

"You aren't looking for a red-haired lady, are you?" says the male tourist. "We saw her. She ran through to the stairs!"

"Thanks!" you tell him. "Zack, we can take the elevator to wherever she's going and get there first."

Zack grins. "I figure there's only three places she could be headed. The underground parking level, the roof, or my penthouse suite. There's information about the tomb on my laptop, and she'd love to get her hands on it." He reaches out for the elevator button.

To ride the elevator all the way up to the roof, go to page 127.

To visit Zack's penthouse suite, go to page 120.

To head to the parking lot instead, go to page 134.

You hide. And you wait. And you wait, and you wait . . .

After half an hour, you hear an approaching vehicle. Finally! You tense up, expecting something exciting to happen. But it goes straight past the ruins and keeps going. It was nothing but a soft-drink delivery truck.

Zack sighs. "We've been played," he explains.

Scarlett must have realized you were tailing her, and faked the cell phone call just so she could send you out here on a wild goose chase. She is supposed to be a corporate super-spy, after all.

Oh well, you've only lost a couple of hours. Back to the hotel you go . . .

Head to page 92.

120

You take the elevator up to Zack's suite. On the way, the tourists figure out who he is and are all smiles by the time you leave. Zack is super nice and gives all of them autographs, though he knows there isn't time.

You look around anxiously for Scarlett, but there's no sign of her. Wherever she was heading, this wasn't it. "We'll never catch her now," you sigh. "I wonder what she was looking for?"

Zack shrugs. "Guess we'll never know. Come on, kid. Let's chill for a while."

Getting to hang out with Zack takes the sting out of losing Scarlett. You drink slushies, watch the sports channels, and play video games on a television the size of the wall. If your friends back home could see you now, they'd explode with envy!

The next morning, you head out to the dig.

Go to page 52.

The stealthy approach pays off. You follow Scarlett through the hotel corridors, ducking around corners and lurking in doorways. She glances over her shoulder from time to time, but you don't think she's noticed you.

You freeze. Her cell phone's ringing. It's some lame old Britpop girl-power ringtone. She answers it. "Fifteen minutes," she says instantly. "The ruins. I'll be there, by the third statue. Make sure you're not followed."

She tucks her phone away and starts briskly walking again.

Zack's excited. "I know where she's heading!" he tells you. "There's a pretty famous ruin to the south of here. It'd only take fifteen minutes to drive. Let's get there first and set an ambush!"

But you've seen enough spy movies to be suspicious. "It might be a trick," you tell him.

"I don't think so. You stay here if you want. I'm going to those ruins no matter what."

122

Zack seems confident he's right. You don't have to go along with his plan, though. If you want, you can stay on Scarlett's tail as long as you can.

If you want to drive out to the ruins with Zack and ambush Scarlett, head to page 124.

If you want to keep tailing Scarlett on your own while Zack drives to the ruins by himself, head to page 135.

You run and vault over the wall, expecting to knock some lurking assassin to the ground. Or possibly even Scarlett herself.

But there's nobody here—nobody human, anyway. The noise from behind the wall was coming from a cobra, slithering over the dry sand on a stone plinth. You land directly on its tail.

Try to see this from the cobra's point of view, OK? It was just slithering along, minding its own business, not hurting anyone, and then suddenly you came vaulting over the wall and stomped on it.

It bites you. Can you blame it, honestly?

You have to take a rain check on the tomb opening, on account of being dead. It's a pretty solid excuse for missing an appointment. It's not much fun, though!

RUN AGAIN? TURN TO PAGE **4**

Zack drives you out in his luxurious rented car with white leather seats and a thumping sound system. You head down a lonely desert trail to the moonlit ruin of an ancient palace.

The pair of you walk out across the open courtyard. Your shadows are long and ghostlike in the moonlight. Huge statues look down at you with blank stone eyes.

There's no sign of Scarlett . . . yet. You have to wonder why she said she was heading out to a place as empty and lonely as this. There's nobody here to meet her, not that you can see, anyway.

"Care for a date?" Zack says.

"Um, what?"

Zack holds out a tray of dates dusted with sugar. "They're tasty."

You and Zack munch dates—which are delicious—and talk about what your next move should be.

"We should stick to the plan," Zack says. "Let's

find somewhere to hide, so when Scarlett turns up we can ambush her."

"*If* she turns up," you add, still thinking of spy movies. "Maybe we should explore this place and make sure no one's already waiting to ambush *us*."

Zack frowns. "That's possible, I guess. Scarlett's a tricky customer. We're going to have to be careful here."

To stick to the original plan, hide in the ruins and wait for Scarlett, go to page 129.

To explore the ruins and the surrounding sand dunes, just in case someone's lying in wait for you, turn to page 130.

You see a steady light in the distance and realize it's one of the floodlights the film crew uses. They must be doing some night filming at the tomb entrance. Won't they be surprised to see you! You stagger from the cave mouth toward them.

Congratulations! You've escaped the buried pyramid of peril and returned safely with a priceless treasure. Even better, the TV cameras are there to record the historic moment!

The idol is transferred to the Museum of Cairo, where you get to go and see it anytime you like. Zack Wonder is proud of you, and gives you a full-time job as the host of his TV show. Stardom awaits!

You think this is probably the best ending you could have hoped for, but you're still curious to know how things might have gone differently. What if you'd chosen different paths along the way? What secrets are still to be discovered?

RUN AGAIN? TURN TO PAGE **4**

You arrive on the rooftop, and there's Scarlett! You're just in time to see her pulling out some sort of pistol-like device. You hesitate. She's not going to shoot you, is she? You get ready to dodge.

Phew—it's only a zip-line launcher. Scarlett fires, and a tiny grappling hook on a super-tough cable goes whizzing across to the next building. She tugs the cable to make sure it's secure, then fastens it at her end.

Scarlett zip-lines across to the building next door, a multistory parking lot. She's getting away, just when you thought you had her cornered!

You could chase after her, if you had something to loop over the zip-line and protect your hands. Zack has the same idea and unfastens a thick gold chain from around his neck for you to use to swing over the line and zip down on. "Get after her, kid!"

"You're not coming?"

Zack jerks a thumb at the zip-line. "That bitty little line won't take my weight. I'd be a pizza on the sidewalk if I tried to cross."

128

You run to the edge of the rooftop and look down the length of the line, winding the gold chain hesitantly around your left hand. It's a long way down. This is scary. Maybe there's a safer option?

Of course! You could take the elevator back down to the underground parking level—it's connected to the building opposite—and catch Scarlett that way. If you were quick, you could probably make it. But the zip-line would be faster, for sure . . .

To zip-line across and sprint down after Scarlett, head to page 135.

To play it safe and take the elevator down to the underground parking level, zoom to page 134.

It doesn't take you long to find a shallow pit where you could hunker down and wait for Scarlett. It's just below a worn statue of a goddess who looks like she has a strange, many-legged creature on her head. A spider? No, the body's too long for that. It looks like it has a curved tail, though.

But Zack points out a row of weathered pillars instead. They must have been spectacular once, but now they just look like big, broken stumps. You and Zack could pick a pillar each and hide behind them, only looking out when you think it's safe.

Choose your hiding place!

To hide in the pit by the strange goddess statue, head to page 105.

To hide behind the worn-down pillars, head to page 119.

"We'd better check this place out," you tell Zack. "Scarlett could be setting us up."

Zack nods. "Yeah, that'd be in her nature."

Moving cautiously, you and Zack explore the site. You have to admit, these ruins are cool. There are hieroglyphic inscriptions, statues, sphinxes, and pillars. The remains of the walls show you how huge and impressive it must have been years ago.

Suddenly, you hear a noise from behind a wall. It's a gritty, sliding sound, like someone shifting position on a sandy surface. Zack hears it, too. He looks to you, an eyebrow raised.

What do you do? Do you leap over the wall and take whoever (or *whatever*) it is by surprise? Or do you head round the wall one way while Zack goes the other, and try to trap them between you?

To vault over the wall and do a surprise attack, head to page 123.

To come at the mysterious noise from two directions at once, head to page 132.

Scarlett drives you as close to the tomb as she dares. "You've made a smart choice," she says. "Just be careful, OK? Don't go stirring anything up."

"Stirring what up?" you ask nervously.

"Just be careful," she repeats, and drops you off.

You look down into an open pit. You see a little pyramid down there. It's obviously been dug out recently. This is the tomb you and Guy were supposed to be exploring tomorrow. It doesn't look very big.

There are no security guards on patrol nearby, despite what Scarlett said. Nobody sees you as you break the seal on the tomb door and slip inside.

You flick on your flashlight and gasp at the wonders inside the tomb. Wall paintings, grave goods, mummy cases . . . and stairs leading down. You fire up Scarlett's electronic mapping device and follow the directions.

Eventually, the device guides you to a secret temple right in the heart of the tomb. You switch off the device and take a good look around.

Head to page 114.

Using only hand gestures, you tell Zack the plan. He nods, understanding you completely.

You and Zack get ready to jump on whoever the bad guy behind the wall is. This is great—it's like you're on the football field together!

You're just rounding the corner when you hear him yell, "STOP!"

That's when you see the cobra writhing across the stones. You think of what could have happened if you'd leapt over the wall and landed on it, and you shudder.

Zack wipes the sweat from his forehead. "Kid, I think that was a sign. We are not meant to be here tonight. We should cut our losses and go back to the hotel."

"But what about Scarlett?" you say.

"She must have known we were tailing her all along!" Zack says, shaking his head.

"She only mentioned these ruins because she knew we'd come out here."

Zack's pretty convincing, and you have just escaped a possibly fatal cobra bite, which probably used up all your luck for one day. Maybe you'd better save the rest of your luck for tomorrow?

If you want to head back to the hotel,
go to page 52.

If you'd rather stick to the plan, hide and wait
for Scarlett to arrive, head to page 129.

You arrive in the parking lot seconds too late. You look around for Scarlett and hear a car engine revving. There she is, pulling out of the parking lot in a black sports car. She gives you a little wave, which makes Zack furious.

There's nothing to do but to head back to your rooms and wait for tomorrow's dig.

Head to page 92.

You follow Scarlett all the way down to the underground parking lot. You're out of breath by the time you finally reach her. You badly want to take a rest stop, but you don't want to let her out of your sight, so you keep going.

Scarlett slips over to a gleaming black sports car and starts the ignition. She looks up and sees you.

"You're alone?" she says, surprised. You nod.

"Get in!" she shouts.

"What?"

"You want answers, then you can have them. But not here!"

You jump in and buckle up. Scarlett drives out of the hotel, through the streets, and into the desert.

You pull up under some palm trees beside the Nile, under a bright moon. It looks like Scarlett wants to talk this through. "Sorry about leading you on a merry chase back at the hotel," she says. "I couldn't talk to you there, because corporate spies could be listening in. Rival ones."

You think about spy movies again and put two

and two together. That's what she was doing with the electronic device—scanning for bugs!

"So what's so important?" you ask her. "And how come you can tell me, but not Zack?"

She laughs. "Zack Wonder is a good guy. That's the problem. He's too much of a good guy, and he's too well-known. I need someone who can get their hands dirty. Shall I go on?"

"OK," you answer, just so you can find out what her deal is.

"The newly discovered tomb," she says, "contains a priceless golden idol of incredible power. Other archaeologists might not have recognized the hieroglyphs, but I certainly have. I've seen images like that before!"

You decide to let her keep talking.

"Now, I know smuggling artifacts out of the country is shady work, but my corporate bosses are putting a lot of pressure on me to bring the idol back for them, and I just can't let them down. So I want to make a deal with you."

"What kind of a deal?" you ask, suspicious.

"I haven't the slightest chance of getting inside that tomb. Too much security. But you're the star of Zack's show. They'll let you walk right in anytime you want!"

The shoe drops. "You want me to get the golden idol for you?"

"Bright kid," Scarlett says with a half-smile. "I can provide you with a high-tech electronic map of the inside of the buried tomb—I've been able to scan it from a distance using my clever little gadgets—and it will lead you straight to the hidden central burial chamber."

Scarlett tells you her terms. Get in, get the idol, and bring it to her so it can be stored safely, and she'll make it worth your while. "My employers are very rich people," she says. "Did you ever want something extra special for your birthday? A really *big* present? Something you knew you could never have, because it would cost so much? Well, now you can."

She gives you her cell number so you can call

her when you have the idol: (919) 205-8357. *Make a note of Scarlett's number—this is important.*

A thought strikes you. Even if you accept Scarlett's offer, you don't have to give her the idol, right? You could even double-cross *her* . . .

To take Scarlett up on her offer and follow the high-tech electronic map to the hidden burial chamber, turn to page 131.

To reject Scarlett's plan outright, head back to the hotel instead, and go to the dig tomorrow, turn to page 52.

You rush toward the demon monkey, yelling at the top of your voice. The creature rushes at you, yelling even louder. A hulking demon monkey with a skull for a head isn't really going to be scared by loud noises, you realize as it grabs you in its huge claws. You make a leathery meal.

RUN AGAIN? TURN TO PAGE **4**

The demon monkey stops in its tracks. You think it looks alarmed. Maybe it wasn't expecting its prey to fight back? With the idol under your arm, you hack and slash at the air with the ancient Egyptian sword. Good workmanship on this thing—it's lasted for centuries and there's still an edge on it!

You advance on the demon monkey, which backs away from you. Then an evil look comes over its bandaged face. You're sure it's going to leap at you in a surprise attack and try to smash you to the ground.

Maybe you should run while you still can! Or you could drop the idol and hold the sword in a fearsome two-handed grip, bracing yourself for the demon monkey to leap. The sword is strong enough to do some damage, you think. At least you're pretty sure.

To turn and run for your life, go to page 144.

To stand and brace yourself to meet the demon monkey's attack, head to page 143.

You leap the pit easily. Unfortunately, directly after the lousy pit trap is a much better concealed pit trap. Because you jumped with all your strength, you go flying into it.

The demon monkey looks down at you and laughs in a nasty way. Looks like you're not going anywhere for a while.

This is bad. You're trapped in an ancient Egyptian tomb with a hideous beast waiting to eat you. A rescue team might be coming . . . or it might not.

You sigh. With nothing else to do but pass the time down here, you get your phone out and start playing a game. The demon monkey squats at the edge of the pit and watches you curiously. You swipe and tilt your phone, trying to pretend it's not there.

You lose a couple of lives. The demon monkey jumps up and down angrily. It beats its chest and makes a bellowing noise. "Oh, you think you could do better?" you tell it.

The monkey grunts and goes back to watching

you. You get the strong impression it wants a chance to play.

At least the time's passing more quickly now. Of course, in a while you'll run out of battery charge, but that's something you'll just have to worry about later . . .

RUN AGAIN? TURN TO PAGE **4**

The demon monkey jumps. You roar like a barbarian and swing the sword at it. The sword slams down on the demon monkey's skull, and the blade shatters into pieces.

Stunned, the demon monkey wobbles back and forth before falling to the ground with a heavy thump.

You grab the idol and get out of there. You sure don't want to be hanging around when the monkey wakes up!

You sprint through a broad gallery whose ceiling is held up by lotus-patterned columns, leap over a badly concealed pit, and then narrowly avoid falling into a much better concealed pit. You're dodging out of the way of some spear traps when you hear the furious roar of the demon monkey behind you. It's awake, and it's angry!

Sprint to page 146.

With the demon monkey close on your heels, you run from the burial chamber into a broad, pillared gallery.

Up ahead, you can see what looks like a pit in the floor, which some ancient tomb builder has covered up with badly painted planks. If it's supposed to be a trap, it's not a very good one.

At the speed you're going, you could jump it easily. Or you could swerve to avoid it, which would mean slowing down and possibly being grabbed by the demon monkey.

If you want to leap over the pit with all your strength, jump to page 141.

If you'd rather run around the side of the pit and risk the demon monkey catching you, turn to page 147.

Not long afterward, Scarlett arrives in her flashy black sports car. You make the transaction, but you're not sure you can trust Scarlett to keep up her end of the deal. She promises you that your reward is coming. You'll just have to be patient.

After the filming, you travel back home. To your amazement, you discover that Scarlett has made you a present of a gorgeous black car just like hers. It even has a cuddly fox mascot dangling from the mirror. There's a paper speech bubble taped to the fox's muzzle.

CHECK THE TRUNK. S. XX

The trunk is full of the latest video games, a case of chocolate bars, and tickets for a family vacation in Bermuda. You have to admit, as far as "birthday presents" go, it's impressive.

Of course, you can't drive the car yet. Your parents insist you get your license first. And that could be years away. But you do get to look at it every morning, parked in your driveway, and sigh . . .

RUN AGAIN? TURN TO PAGE **4**

146

You skid around a corner and charge down another corridor. The demon monkey is right behind you, bellowing.

This corridor is partially collapsed, with piles of rubble to the left and right. You have to jump over them so as not to go stumbling. Up ahead, you see stairs leading down.

Run to page 79.

You dodge around the pit. The demon monkey's footsteps thunder behind you. It's close, you can tell. You glance over your shoulder, only to see it lunging at you with an outstretched claw.

If that claw catches you, you're finished!

To duck out of the way, head to page 149.

To put on a burst of speed and try to escape the claw that way, leap to page 150.

This chamber is lined with mummies, and it's a dead end. It gives you an uncomfortable feeling. You are about to leave when you notice something odd.

On looking closer, you can't help but think they look like mummified monkeys. They have large chests and long heads, and they're hunched over. But that can't be right, can it? The Egyptians didn't mummify monkeys, did they?

As you watch, you are certain one of the mummies twitches slightly.

To get a closer look, turn to page 83.

To get out of there and go the other way, turn to page 81.

You duck out of the path of the demon monkey's claw and keep running. You also manage to avoid a cunningly concealed pit trap at the last minute.

What is with all these pit traps? It's like the ancient Egyptian tomb builders kept thinking, "Hmm, you know what we really need here, Imhotep? A nice pit. It'll really tie the tomb together."

You shake your head and keep running.

Head to page 146.

Y ou glance back again, put on a burst of speed, and charge right into a cunningly concealed pit. As the trapdoor bangs shut above your head, you hear the demon monkey bellowing. It scrabbles to open the trapdoor, but its huge claws can't manage it.

Well, at least you aren't being eaten by a demon monkey. But you are trapped in a tiny pit with no way out. What's more, there are bugs down here, crawling all over the floor and walls.

Wow. These critters are an amazingly bright purple. Spiky, too—you just stepped on one and it hurt. They need a cool name, like "Ultra Beetles."

If you ever make it out of this tomb, you'll be famous for finding a new species of insect. As you listen to the demon monkey stomping around above, though, you wonder how likely escape really is.

Maybe you could train the Ultra Beetles to be your own private army . . .

RUN AGAIN? TURN TO PAGE **4**

Y ou place your hands against the statue and push. To your amazement, you trigger some kind of mechanism. A stone slab comes grinding down from the ceiling and closes off the doorway completely.

The demon monkey bellows and pounds on the slab, but you don't think he's going to get through in a hurry. *Phew!*

You start climbing down the chain.

Head to page 154.

152

You've barely started climbing down when the demon monkey bursts into the room. He pulls up the chain, revealing you clinging to it like a spider on a bath plug. Do we really need to spell out what happens next?

RUN AGAIN? TURN TO PAGE **4**

Y ou call Scarlett. "You've got the idol?" she practically squeals at you. "You little genius! Sit tight, I'll be right there. Don't move!"

Now you just have to wait for her to arrive. You've got a few moments to think things over while you wait.

Trying to smuggle artifacts out of the country isn't exactly what heroes do. Now that you really think about it, you're not sure you want to go through with it, whatever kind of reward Scarlett's offering. You could call Zack Wonder and get him to bring the police, in order to have Scarlett arrested when she turns up.

Then again, you took the risks, and you've got the idol, so it's totally up to you what you do with it.

To call Zack Wonder and arrange for Scarlett to be arrested, head to page 89.

If you just want to wait for her and go through with the deal, turn to page 145.

As you lower yourself down the chain, the neat blocks around you give way to roughly worked stone. The shaft levels off, and you find yourself crawling down a natural channel through the rock. You're out of the tomb, but you're not sure where you are. It seems like some sort of cave system.

Cool air blows in your face. That's a fantastic sign. It means there's a way back to the surface! You wet your finger and try to find out which way the breeze is coming from. After heading down a few dead ends, you soon find yourself in a sandy-floored cavern.

Are those stars high overhead? You rub your eyes and look again. You must have been inside that tomb for hours! Almost home and dry now. You tuck the idol firmly under your arm and climb up the cavern walls, pulling yourself up and up until you finally collapse, exhausted, on the sandy desert floor. You did it! You're out of that tomb of nightmares, and what's more, you've got a valuable prize—the golden idol you're still clutching tightly.

The question is, what do you do with the idol

now? Depending on who you've talked to on this run so far, someone might have promised you a great big "birthday present" for bringing the idol to them. Perhaps you're eager to get your hands on this birthday present—after all, the idol's nice to look at, but it's not much use to you, is it?

Then again, you might not want to give up the idol, no matter what the price.

If you want to call a certain mysterious redhead, turn to page 153.

If you don't know who this mysterious person is, or you *don't* want to call them, turn to page 126.